A New Home
for Jake

Also available in this series:

A New Home for Jake

Linda Jennings
illustrated by Kate Aldous

MAGI PUBLICATIONS

for Shirin, Billy and Cameron
LJ

for Max
KA

First published in Great Britain 2002 by
LITTLE TIGER PRESS
1 The Coda Centre,
189 Munster Road, London SW6 6AW
www.littletigerpress.com

Text © Little Tiger Press, 2002
Illustrations © Kate Aldous, 2002

A CIP catalogue record for this book
is available from the British Library

Printed and bound in Great Britain
by Bookmarque Ltd.
Set in 16.8pt Goudy

1 3 5 7 9 10 8 6 4 2

Contents

Chapter One

"Will I always live here with you, Mum?" asked Jake.

His mother looked down at him. He was a plump little pony with dark, dreamy eyes.

"Not always, no," she answered. "When you are older, you'll begin a new life somewhere else."

Jake didn't like the sound of this. He wanted to stay in the quiet meadow. He loved his mum and his friend,

Willow the old racehorse, who shared the meadow with them. When Willow was younger she had galloped with other horses down a long track to the winning post.

"There's nothing quite like racing," she had told Jake. "The feel of the wind rushing through your mane, the thundering of the other horses' hooves as you overtake them, and the cheers from the crowd as you win. I've been in the newspapers, you know. I was famous once."

Even now Willow could run really fast.

"Wow!" called Jake, his eyes shining, as the big horse thundered round the field. "What a speed. I wish I could run like you!"

He tried sometimes, but he could never catch up with her.

"I want to be a racehorse when I grow up," Jake told his mum.

"Don't be daft," Mum snorted.

"Racehorses are tall and long-legged. Your legs are too short. You're a pony, not a horse."

"A race *pony*, then?"

"Willow has filled your head with a lot of silly nonsense," said Mum. "You must forget all about racehorses. You'll be going to a nice home with a little boy or girl to ride you."

"No races?"

"Perhaps a gymkhana. That's a pony competition. Trotting in line, jumping fences, that sort of thing."

It sounded a bit boring to Jake.

"Race you!" he called out to Willow who was grazing nearby.

"Not now, little pony," sighed Willow. "I need my afternoon rest."

* * *

In the early spring, a leather halter was put round Jake's head, and a nasty metal bit placed in his mouth.

"I don't like it, Mum," he complained, tossing his head and trying to spit the bit out.

"Be patient," said his mum. "You'll get used to it. All ponies and horses do."

"Did Willow?"

"Yes, of course she did. Racehorses have *very* strict training."

Next, a saddle was placed over Jake's back, along with a girth, wrapped around his tummy to keep the saddle in place. Two leather straps with metal stirrups on the end hung down on either side.

It wasn't long before Jake was

"broken in". This meant the farmer thought he was ready to be ridden. But when the farmer's daughter, Becky, climbed into the saddle, Jake neighed with shock and tried to throw her off.

"Steady, Jake," said Mum. "You must learn to take a rider. It's what ponies do – and racehorses."

Jake soon learned that if he did as he was told, the farmer would reward him with sugar lumps and pieces of crunchy carrot. Gradually, he became used to Becky riding him round the meadow. He began to enjoy it.

Then one day, when Willow was galloping by on her morning exercise, Jake tried to race along beside her with Becky on his back. Willow outpaced him, and Jake gathered speed. "I *will* be a race pony," he panted. "Just you see!"

"Whoa!" shouted Becky, pulling at Jake's reins. "Slow down."

"Ouch!" went Jake, as the bit dug into his mouth.

He reared up, and Becky hung on tight.

"Naughty pony," she scolded. "Don't you ever do that again."

And for a while Jake didn't. He hated the feel of that iron bit.

Chapter Two

A few weeks later, when the young green leaves were unfurling on the trees, a man came into the meadow with the farmer. He opened Jake's mouth and looked at his teeth, he examined his legs and hooves. Then he nodded and shook the farmer's hand.

"That's your new owner," Jake's mum said. "I think he likes you."

Jake began to panic. "Am I going away, then?"

"Yes, Jake, you are. A new life for you. It will be fun!"

"But I don't want a new life," Jake said. "I don't want to leave you and Willow."

Jake's mum nuzzled him, and she whispered in his ear. "Be brave, Jake. Every little pony has to leave home one day. But listen to me. Don't look back. Don't dream of racehorses, or even of your old home. Look forward to the excitement of something new!"

"But Mum –"

"Behave yourself, Jake, wherever you go. And none of your silly tricks."

Jake was led away across the meadow.

"Goodbye!" his mother called after him. "Remember what I've said."

Willow cantered along beside him.

"Good luck!" she called. "We won't forget you!"

Jake was bumped and rattled along the road in a horse box. He felt frightened and lost. He looked out of the little window at the side as the countryside whizzed by.

Where was he going? What would his life be like now?

At last the horse box stopped and the doors were opened. Nervously, Jake backed down the ramp and into a small stable yard. He blinked. From every open stable door poked an inquisitive pony head.

"Hello," said a white pony with a black patch over one eye. "Are you the new beach pony?"

Beach pony? What was that?

Jake looked around and didn't like what he saw. The yard was terribly untidy. It had been raining, and there were large puddles of water everywhere.

The wooden stables should have been white, but the paint was peeling. There was a strange smell in the air, too, that made Jake's nose twitch and his hooves tingle.

"Don't worry," said the white pony, when she saw Jake's expression. "All ponies feel homesick at first. But it's nice here, and Tom feeds us well. Living by the sea is brilliant."

"Huh," snorted a depressed looking brown pony. "Just wait till there's a gale. Then the wind blows across the bay and salt gets into your pony food."

The next morning, after Jake had been brushed and his hooves polished, the stable girl saddled him up. Then she and Tom led him with the other seven ponies out of the yard, through a field and into a lane. It was a bright, sunny morning, but Conker, the brown pony, was still grumbling.

"It's go, go, go, all the summer," he said. "Up and down the beach, horrible kids on your back . . ."

"Don't take any notice," Jess, the white pony, told Jake. "Nothing's ever right for Conker. And the children are lovely. You'll see."

The ponies walked slowly up the hill in a long line. Once, Jake stopped to crop some grass, but a quick tug at his reins told him he had to follow the others.

At the top of the hill, though, Jake stopped suddenly and stared. Ahead of him was a huge expanse of blue water.

It glittered in the sunshine, and at the edge was a frothy white line.

"What's that?" he asked Jess.

"The sea!" said Jess. "Look at that golden beach! Isn't it the loveliest thing you've ever seen?"

"Come *on*, Jake," said Tom, pulling at Jake's rein. "Get a move on!"

The ponies made their way down the steep lane towards the beach. Jake couldn't help feeling excited. He could see everything properly now. The beach stretched for miles. People were putting up chairs and settling down on rugs. Children were playing in the white foam at the edge of the water.

The air smelled different here, too. It was salty and tangy, and it made Jake feel suddenly excited and happy. How he longed to gallop along that beach!

Chapter Three

The ponies gathered by a little hut. A crowd of small children was already waiting, chattering and laughing and pointing.

"I'd like to ride that spotty white one!"

"I want my favourite black one!"

"There's a new pony – look!"

Jake found himself surrounded by children. They patted his nose, and one gave him a sugar lump.

Several wanted to ride him straight away.

Jake felt nervous. He had been trained by Becky, but had never been ridden by anyone else.

Tom helped a little fair-haired girl on to Jake's back.

"Don't tug at the reins unless I tell you to," he told her. "I'll be leading you. You'll be quite safe."

"What's his name?" the little girl wanted to know.

"Jake," said Tom. "He came here yesterday. He's a great little pony, isn't he?"

The little girl nodded happily. She took Jake's reins gently, and they were off, plodding along behind the other ponies.

After a few metres Jake began to feel impatient. But when he tried to trot, Tom told the little girl to pull him back. They reached the pier and the ponies turned round. They walked, all too slowly, back again.

"Can't we go any further?" Jake called to Jess. "There's so much room here. Why can't we gallop across the sands?"

"Because we're beach ponies. Beach ponies never gallop. We keep in line, and we never go further than the pier."

The little girl dismounted and another child climbed on Jake's back. Off they went again.

By the middle of the morning, Jake was bored. Was this what his new life was all about? He thought of his mum and Willow and wished with all his heart that he was with them.

"*Never look back*," his mum had told him. But how could he help it, when all he had to look forward to were days and days of plodding to and fro along a wonderful beach that was made for galloping?

At the end of the day, the ponies were rubbed down, groomed and given their supper.

"Cheer up," Jess told Jake. "You'll get used to things. It's a nice peaceful life."

"*But I don't want a nice peaceful life!*" thought Jake. "*I want to be a race pony!*"

Day followed day, and Jake walked up and down the beach, carrying children to the pier and back. When a little girl dug her heels into Jake's sides, and said "Gee up!", Tom tightened the rein to hold him back. But mostly the children were very small and only wanted a gentle ride across the sands.

Chapter Four

One morning, Jake spotted a slim, long-legged pony by the edge of the sea. It reminded him of Willow.

As the line of beach ponies made their way to the pier, Jake saw it take off along the beach with a girl on its back. Clumps of sand flew in the air as it gathered speed and splashed in and out of the water.

Jake's feet felt fidgety, and he thought of Willow and the stories of her racing days. Before anyone knew what was happening, Jake left the line of ponies and began to gallop!

The little boy riding Jake clung to his neck, trying to stop himself from falling off. Jake had only gone a few metres before Tom caught him.

"You bad pony!" he yelled, flicking his rein on Jake's tender nose. "How *dare* you do that!"

Tom helped the little boy down. The child's mother cried angrily at Tom, "That pony's dangerous! Hasn't it been properly trained?"

"He has," said Tom. "He doesn't usually do this, but he's a young pony, and I guess he got a bit too excited."

But the little boy was laughing. He seemed pleased that he hadn't fallen off Jake's back.

"Perhaps he wants to gallop, too!" thought Jake.

* * *

Jake was in disgrace. When the other ponies left for the beach that afternoon, Jake stayed behind in the field.

Jess looked worried. "Tom doesn't like frisky ponies," she told him. "You must learn not to get so excited."

Conker nodded gloomily. "Tom will probably get rid of you now," he said. "And then, goodness knows where you'll go."

The ponies walked through the field past Jake and into the lane.

"Don't worry!" Jess called back. "I expect Tom will give you some more training."

Training! Jake didn't *want* to be trained to plod along the beach for the rest of his life.

As the clip-clop of the ponies' hooves faded, Jake stood in the middle of the field, pawing impatiently.

"They've left you here all alone, have they?" called the stable cat.

Jake sighed. "It's no good," he said. "I don't like being a beach pony. It's dead boring."

"I agree with you," said the cat. "I'd go mad if I couldn't come and go as I please. Once I was shut in a shed by mistake. Horrible!"

"But what shall I do? If Tom gets rid of me, I may end up somewhere even worse!"

"You could escape. It's not difficult. The gate's quite low, and you could jump it."

"Then what?" asked Jake.

"You could have an adventure, silly. You could follow your dreams."

Jake thought of the pony on the beach. He thought of the long stretch of golden sand. He thought of the row of rocks jutting out into the bay. What lay behind them? He didn't know, because he had only ever gone in the other direction, as far as the pier. Now was his chance to find out!

Although Jake had galloped in the field with Willow, he had never jumped a gate before.

"Give yourself plenty of room," advised the cat. "Start off from the other end of the field and then run towards the gate, really fast."

Jake did as the cat said, but when he saw the gate looming up in front of him, he stopped short. He was too frightened to jump.

"Chicken!" called the cat.

Jake tried again and again. He wished his little legs weren't so short. He wished he wasn't so fat.

"Made it!" he shouted, when he'd tried for the fourth time. He just scraped the top bar of the gate with his back feet as he sailed over.

He skidded to a halt in the middle of the lane.

"Brilliant!" called the cat. "Now the whole world is yours. Make the best of it."

"I will," said Jake, setting off hopefully.

Chapter Five

The cat followed Jake to the top of the hill, then stopped.

"I won't come any further," she said. "I don't fancy the sea. Cats don't like getting their paws wet."

"I'm on my own now," thought Jake. A little shiver of excitement went through him. Now he could do exactly as he wanted! He could gallop like a racehorse. Perhaps someone would see him speeding along the sands. He would become the best race pony in the country. He would win prizes. He would be famous!

Jake trotted eagerly down the hill, but then stopped suddenly. If he went down to the beach, Tom would spot him at once.

Jake waited till he saw the ponies walking towards the pier. Then he made his way quickly down to the beach, and set off in the opposite direction.

The sea spangled in the sun, with little dancing waves at its edge, covered in lacy foam. Jake rushed straight in, splashing droplets of water everywhere. They flew up, and some stung him in the eye.

Jake shook his head and spluttered.

"The sea's not as nice as it looks," he thought, jumping back on to the beach, which stretched in every direction like a giant field. At the end of the bay was the row of rocks, cutting the beach off from the next bay.

"I can get there in a couple of shakes of a pony's tail," Jake thought. Off he galloped, faster and faster. Oh, it was a great feeling, with the sea breeze blowing in his mane. He reached the row of rocks, turned round and began to gallop back.

Jake forgot he was on the beach. He was at the races, speeding past other, slower horses towards the winning post. He could see them all in a long line, out of the corner of his eye.

"*Oi!*" Someone was calling him, loudly and angrily!

Jake skidded to a stop, sending a shower of sand into his eyes. Suddenly, he remembered where he was.

On the beach. The ponies hadn't been horses in a race. They were the beach

ponies, standing in a row, staring at him
in amazement. Tom was there, too.

"You stay right there!" he called,
running towards Jake.

Jake panicked. Tom was mad with
him. He'd take him back to the field,

then sell him. "*Goodness knows where you'll go*," Conker had said.

"Right now," Jake thought, "I must get away from Tom."

Jake wheeled round and sped off back towards the row of rocks.

"Run, pony, run!" he heard someone cry as he flashed past. Jake couldn't be sure, but it looked very like the little boy who had almost fallen off his back!

Now that he was near the rocks, Jake saw that he could get round them and into the next bay by a very narrow strip of sand. Very carefully, Jake picked his way along it. Far in the distance, he could hear Tom's angry shouts and the little boy's excited cries.

Chapter Six

The next bay was tiny. The sea swirled round Jake's feet, and he didn't like the feel of it. He scrambled up the little beach to where it was dry, but the water rushed after him. The tide was coming in fast.

At the other end of the bay was a tall cliff, stretching out into the sea.

"There's no way out there," thought Jake. "I'm trapped!"

Wave by wave, the sea covered the

sand. Jake was frightened. The little bit of sand on which he stood had now shrunk to nothing, and he was leg-deep in cold salt water. It was creeping up, higher and higher.

Where was Tom? Why hadn't he followed Jake into the bay?

"Perhaps he didn't see me go round the rocks. Perhaps he's looking for me somewhere else," thought Jake.

He tried to walk back the way he had come, but the water was too deep and the current too strong. It was like trying to move through thick mud.

He squashed himself up against the cliff face and gave one loud, alarmed whinny. *"Please come, Tom, before I'm washed away!"*

* * *

Jake shivered and shook as the sea rose
to his tummy. He thought of the lovely
field where he had been born. He
thought of his mum and of Willow.

He even thought of the beach ponies and his scruffy old stable. He wondered if he would ever see Jess or Conker again.

Then, suddenly, Jake heard voices above him, Tom's amongst them. But how could Tom rescue him from the top of a cliff?

There was shouting and, before Jake knew what was happening, he saw Tom dangling just above him on the end of a rope.

"Hang on, little fellow," Tom said. "Don't move."

Swaying in the air, Tom somehow managed to fix a sling round Jake's fat tummy.

"Pull!" he shouted to the people above him.

Jake suddenly found himself in the air, too, swinging back and fro as he was hauled up the cliff.

"Ooh!" he whinnied, as he looked down to the sea swirling beneath him. "I feel sick!"

At last he was on dry land. Tom followed, on his own rope.

Jake expected Tom to be mad with him, but he wasn't.

"You look a right sight," said Tom, rubbing Jake down with a towel. "Now you see what happens when you do as you want to, not what you are supposed to!"

Chapter Seven

Back at the stables, Tom finished drying Jake off and fed him.

"Don't you dare escape again!" he said, shaking his head. "Goodness knows what I'll do with you. You're no beach pony, that's for sure."

When Tom had gone, Jake stood quietly, staring out at the untidy yard. What would happen to him now? He wanted to ask Jess about it, but she was still on the beach with the other ponies.

"Back again, then?" came a familiar voice. "No adventures?"

The stable cat jumped lightly into Jake's stall.

Jake told the cat what had happened, and how he had nearly drowned.

"I didn't want *that* sort of adventure," he said. "I just wanted to win races and be famous."

"Forget it," said the cat. "There are no such things as racing ponies. You need a new owner who likes a bit of excitement. Someone small and bouncy, like yourself."

The cat was right. Jake had followed his dreams, but they hadn't come true. He wasn't meant to be a racing pony after all. He needed something exciting and different – but what?

Jess and Conker wanted to hear all about Jake's adventures when they came back.

"Daft, I call it," grumbled Conker. "All that galloping for freedom. Why not stay with us, safe and sound?"

"It must have been exciting, though," said Jess, her eyes shining. "I've *always* wondered what it was like beyond the beach."

"Well, now you know," said Conker. "Nasty, wet sea, and being hauled up the cliff by your tummy. Ugh!"

Jake wondered what would happen to him. Tom thought he was a useless beach pony, and he was too small and tubby to go racing. Perhaps the cat was right. He just needed an owner who, like himself, wanted a bit of fun.

He settled down for the night, wondering what the next day would bring.

In the morning, when Jess, Conker and the other ponies set off for the beach,

Jake stayed behind in the field. As he walked past with the ponies, Tom stared at him and gave a big sigh.

"We'll have to think what to do about you, little fellow," he said. He gave Jake a friendly pat on his nose. "I'll ask around. You can't stay here."

Jake knew his new home wasn't bad. Tom was kind, and he liked all the ponies. Even Conker was all right, in his grumpy way. And though the stable was untidy, his stall was warm and he had enough to eat.

The sound of the ponies' hooves grew fainter. Jake galloped round and round the field, faster and faster, but there was no one there to admire his efforts.

Or was there?

Chapter Eight

There was the clip-clop of a pony's hooves in the lane. Jake trotted over to the gate, to see who it was.

The hoofbeats stopped, and Jake stared. It was the same chestnut pony who had been galloping along by the sea's edge, and the girl was leading her.

A small boy skipped along ahead. Jake recognised him at once. It was the child who had clung to his neck when Jake had tried to gallop off, the one

who had told him to run when he was
escaping from Tom.

"Look, Kate!" said the little boy. "It's
that pony. The one I rode on the
beach."

"It nearly threw you, Charlie, remember?"

"I don't *care*. He's an ace pony."

Jake didn't understand what they were saying. But he did understand that the little boy thought he was great. Charlie tried to pat Jake's nose through the bars of the gate.

"Careful!" said Kate. "You mustn't touch strange ponies."

"But I like him, Kate. Is he for sale? Mum said I could have a pony, too."

"Not that one. She said that he was dangerous."

Charlie pulled down his mouth and shouted at her. "He's not dangerous! He just wants to gallop, like your Suzie. And I didn't fall off, so there!"

Suzie the chestnut pony stood

watching them. She tossed her head and called across to Jake.

"Charlie's always wanted a pony like you," she said. "Small enough to ride, but lively, too."

Very, very slowly, Charlie stretched out his hand, palm up, and Jake, just as gently, nuzzled it.

"You're right, Charlie," said Kate. "He's not dangerous. He doesn't bite. And he has such gentle eyes."

"You will ask Mum, won't you? You will ask if he's for sale?"

"OK, Charlie, I will," sighed Kate. "But you know what she thinks about him."

When Kate, Charlie and Suzie had gone, Jake felt lonely. He looked forward to the end of the day when Jess, Conker and the others would be home.

The ponies came back earlier than usual.

"Don't know why," said Jess. "There were plenty of children still wanting rides."

"Good thing!" added Conker. "I've got a sore back from all those kids scrambling on and off me."

Tom came out into the field with a brush. "Come on, Jake," he said. "Let's make you look clean and tidy."

Tom brushed Jake's mane and his tail. He looked at his hooves and picked out some small stones. Then he polished them.

"All ready now," he said.

"*Ready for what?*" wondered Jake.

He didn't have to wait for long.

"Look!" shouted Jess. "There's that little boy who you nearly threw, Jake."

"And his mum," added Conker.

"That's bad news. I bet she wants to make trouble."

"Surely you don't want that one, Charlie?" said the woman, coming closer. "Not after what happened to you?"

"Yes I do. He's OK, Mum, honestly he is. He nuzzled my hand."

"Can you trot him round the field for us?" Charlie's mum asked Tom.

"You behave yourself," whispered Tom to Jake as they set off. "No frisky behaviour."

"Well, he *seems* a good little pony," Charlie's mum said as Tom returned, Jake trotting obediently at his side. She stroked Jake on his nose and looked at him thoughtfully. "All right, Charlie, let Tom lead you round now."

Tom lifted Charlie on to Jake's back.

"Gee up!" shouted Charlie, digging his heels into Jake's sides, but Tom shook his head.

"No, Charlie, you should have proper riding lessons before you try to gallop."

Jake longed to gallop round the field with Charlie. He knew the little boy would love it. But out of the corner of his eye he could see Charlie's mum, and something told Jake to be careful. This was a very important moment in his life. There would be plenty of time to gallop when Charlie was ready.

Very quietly and steadily Jake walked round the field again. When Charlie whispered "Gee up" to him once more, he flicked his ear and trotted, just a little quicker. But he didn't gallop.

And when they came back to Charlie's mum, she was smiling and nodding.

The little boy scrambled down and gave Jake some pony nuts on the flat of his hand.

A few minutes later, Charlie gave a big, happy shout and hugged his mother hard. Jake knew he had found a new home and a new beginning.

It was a golden autumn day and the beach was nearly empty. Summer was over and the holidaymakers had gone home.

Along the edge of the sea, the waves danced like frisky horses. Two ponies

were galloping, splashing in and out of
the water. The little tubby one was

trying his best to keep up with his long-legged companion.

"Race you, Suzie," panted Jake.

"Run for it, Jake!" cried Charlie, laughing.